THIS BOOK BELONGS
TO

_____

The Adventures of
Bella & Harry
Let's Visit Jerusalem!

Written By
Lisa Manzione

Illustrated By
Kristine Lucco

Bella & Harry, LLC

www.BellaAndHarry.com
email: BellaAndHarry@mac.com

"**Harry**, be sure to pack your hat for our next adventure with our family!"

"**Why** should I pack my hat, Bella? Where are we going?"

"We are traveling to Jerusalem, Israel. Israel is located right here on our map. Israel is located in an area of the world called the Middle East. The Middle East is very hot during the summer, so you will need your hat and a bottle of water to drink for our tour!"

6

"**Our** first stop is outside of the city of Jerusalem. It is a place called Masada. Harry, did you know the word Masada means fortress in Hebrew?"

"Bella, is that Masada way up on the top of the mountain?"

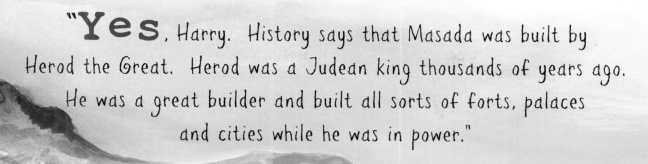

"**Yes**, Harry. History says that Masada was built by Herod the Great. Herod was a Judean king thousands of years ago. He was a great builder and built all sorts of forts, palaces and cities while he was in power."

"Bella, how do we get to the top of the mountain?"

"**Well** Harry, we can take the 'Snake Path'
or we can take the cable car!"

10

"SNAKE PATH!!! Bella, I am scared of snakes!"

"Ha! Ha! Don't worry Harry! It is called the 'Snake Path' because the path has a lot of curves like a snake. It's a long walk up to the top, so I think the children want to take the cable car. Let's go!"

"**Harry**, Masada is one of the most visited sites in Israel. It is believed that not only did Herod the Great build this as his summer palace; another group of people of the Jewish faith lived here too. They were called the Zealots."

"**A** long time ago, the Romans took over the area in Israel where the Zealots lived. The Zealots were very religious and did not want to live with the Romans, so they moved to Masada. Sadly Harry, there are no Zealots remaining now, but their story is still told today."

13

"**Bella**, is that water I see?"

"Yes Harry, it is the Dead Sea."

"The Dead Sea! Bella, that sounds very scary too!"

14

"**NO** Harry, it is called the Dead Sea because it is very salty. The salt prevents life forms from living in the sea. A cool fact is that the Dead Sea shoreline is the lowest place for dry land on earth.

Let's hop on the cable car and head down to the shore. I would love to take a dip in the cool water."

"**WOW!** Bella, look at me! I am floating! This is fun!"

"**Yes** Harry, because of all of the salt in the water, we are floating, not swimming.   Be sure not to drink the water. It tastes yucky!"

"It is time to get out of the water.
Our next stop is the 'Old City' of Jerusalem."

"What does 'Old City' mean Bella?"

"The 'Old City' is just that, Harry. It is the oldest area
in the city of Jerusalem that is surrounded by stone walls.
There are four different areas, or quarters, of the 'Old City'."

18

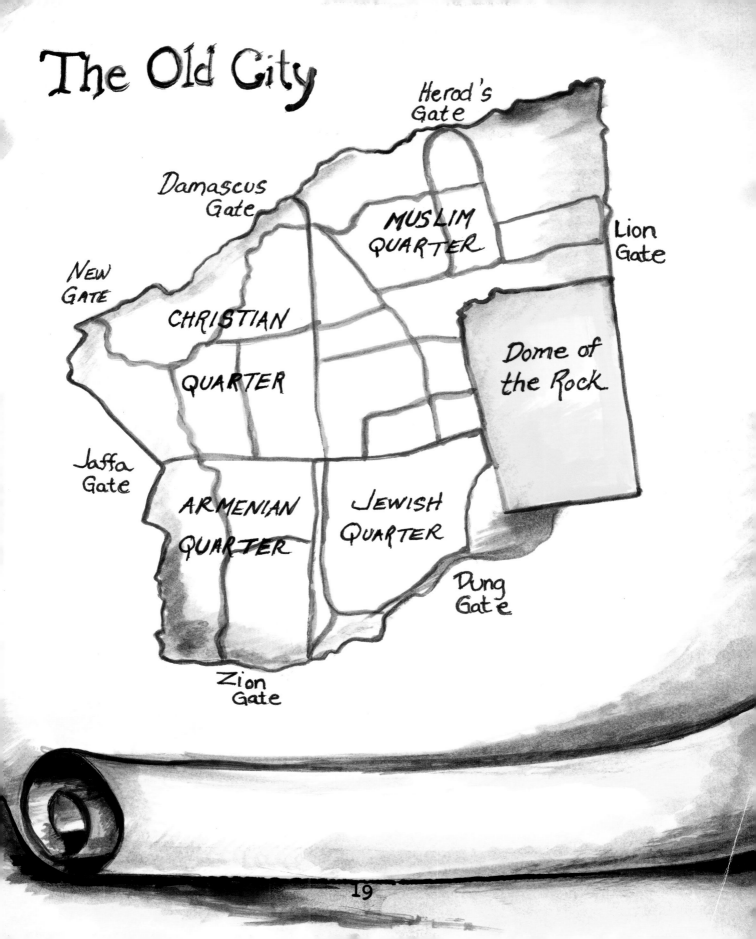

"**Harry**, the four quarters are called the Jewish Quarter, Muslim Quarter, Armenian Quarter and Christian Quarter. The people who live in the different quarters do so because it is a part of their heritage."

"**Harry**, history, heritage and religion are very important to the people who live in Israel."

"**Next** stop is the Jewish Quarter."

22

"**Look** over there Harry! That landmark is called the 'Western Wall', also called the 'Kotel' by some people. It is a large, open air synagogue (a place where people of the Jewish faith go to worship) and can hold thousands of worshipers. Each day prayers take place both day and night for followers of the Jewish faith. It is important to know every faith is welcome to join the worshipers and say their prayers silently, if they want to."

"**The** 'Western Wall' is the holiest of Jewish sites because it is part of the wall that housed the Second Temple. When the Romans took over the city, almost all of the Second Temple was destroyed. The only remaining part is the 'Western Wall'. Many people come from all over the world to place notes inside the cracks of the wall hoping their prayers will be answered."

"**Bella**, was there a First Temple?"

"Yes, Harry. The First Temple was built by King Solomon, son of King David. It was also called Solomon's Temple. It was a place of worship. According to history, the First Temple was extremely beautiful."

"**Bella**, who was King David?"

"King David was one of the most important people in Jewish history. He was king for over 40 years. King David chose Jerusalem as the capital of Israel over 3,000 years ago."

"**Today**, the City of David, which was Jerusalem of ancient times, is located just outside the 'Old City'. The City of David is in ruins now, but we can see what is left of the First and Second Temple era from long ago."

"**Come** on Harry. There is a lot to see in Jerusalem, we can't sit back on our puppy tails today!

Next stop, Hezekiah's Tunnel!"

"Tunnel? Will it be dark? Bella, you know I don't like the dark!"

נקבת חזקיהו

HEZEKIAH'S TUNNEL

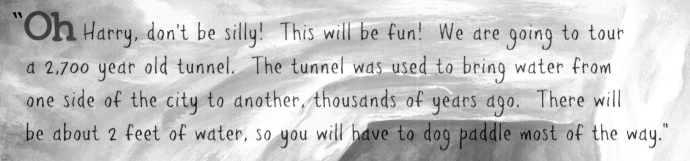

"Oh Harry, don't be silly! This will be fun! We are going to tour a 2,700 year old tunnel. The tunnel was used to bring water from one side of the city to another, thousands of years ago. There will be about 2 feet of water, so you will have to dog paddle most of the way."

"Whew! You are right, Bella! This is a lot of fun!"

"Next stop, dinner!"

"**Bella**, what are the children having for dinner tonight?"

"The children are trying common Israeli food for dinner tonight. It looks like they are having baba ganoush (a traditional eggplant spread), pita bread, shawarma (grilled meat that can be enjoyed with the pita bread) and my very favorite, tahini (a spread made from sesame seeds)! For dessert we are having knafeh, a sweet shredded pastry made with soft cheese!"

"Bella, this looks really good! Yummy!"

Well, dinner is over and it is time to end our tour of Jerusalem. I think we will visit Jerusalem again! There are so many more sights to see. We hope you will join us when we return here but for now it's 'shalom' or good-bye from Bella Boo and Harry too!

32

Our Adventure to Jerusalem

Bella & Harry attending a Bar Mitzvah and listening to a reading from the Torah.

Harry playing backgammon in the 'Old City'.

Bella and Harry enjoying Shabbat dinner.

Bella & Harry placing notes in the Western Wall.

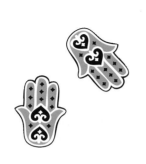

Harry eating a pomelo, also known as a pummelo (a type of citrus fruit).

34

Fun Hebrew Words and Phrases

Shalom -
Hello, Good-bye or Peace

Mazel Tov -
Congratulations

Bevakasha -
Please or You're welcome

Ken - Yes

Lo - No

Boker tov - Good morning

Erev tov - Good evening

Requests for permission to make copies of any part of the work should be directed to BellaAndHarryGo@aol.com or 855-235-5211.

Library of Congress Cataloging-in-Publications Data is available
Manzione, Lisa
The Adventures of Bella & Harry: Let's Visit Jerusalem!

ISBN: 978-1-937616-00-7

First Edition
Book Ten of Bella & Harry Series

For further information please visit:
www.BellaAndHarry.com
or
Email: BellaAndHarryGo@aol.com

CPSIA Section 103 (a) Compliant
www.beaconstar.com/ consumer
ID: L0118329. Tracking No.: MR210171-1-10824
Printed in China